I0710631

THE VAMPIRES COLD CASE

E.H. DRAKE

To my wonderful husband,

The publication of this story is just the beginning of one more dream

you've helped me to realize.

I'll let you guess the first dream.

The ride had turned awkward; my partner kept trying to make small talk while I wanted to discuss work. After a while, we compromised by pretending to listen to the radio. His dark eyes concentrated on the numerous potholes in the road while I stared idly into the inky night beyond the passenger window, reviewing case details in my mind.

I didn't have much to work with. Narcotics had gone in for a big bust and found *something up our alley.* That could mean they found anything from a dead bat to a transfusion bag.

Our unit was still fairly new; we got calls every week and half of them were debunked by the coroner or tech teams before we even arrived. Bureaucracy was still ironing everything out, which meant I was likely sitting through this ridiculous pop song for no reason.

"Seventh time's a charm..." I murmured.

"What's that, buddy?"

Harper had a habit of that; everyone was his buddy or pal. I couldn't decide what his angle was but it wasn't like I could tell him to knock it off. Technically, he was only being friendly.

"Just thinking out loud." I closed my eyes and sat back in the seat. There wasn't much to see out the window in this dark. Not that there was anything to appreciate in the daytime. Daylight would only expose ever-widening cracks in the sidewalk and fast food wrappers imitating tumbleweed in a bad western.

"You do that lot." The sentence was drawn out, implying a question. His large fingers tapped noisily on the steering wheel a couple of times, coercing a response.

"And?" I was so tired of beating around the bush, it was hard to keep the bite from my tone.

The retort hung between us. The methodical tapping of each dark digit held it in place. My body shifted slightly as the car turned onto a new road. "Just wondering what you're like in interviews."

The car halted, giving my body a short, weightless lurch as Harper slammed it into park.

"I know how to keep things to myself." *Otherwise, you'd already know that I've requested a new partner.*

"Good to know," Harpers said with a deep chuckle. I was glad he got out of the car before seeing my scowl.

Harper was probably a decent guy but he was too laid back. I couldn't take him seriously. He wore motorcycle leather every day, even when he drove a car. He joked about anything and everything.

And that chuckle... Was he messing with me? I shook my head, reminding myself it didn't matter.

I straightened my tie as I opened my eyes, taking in the surrounding scene. Through the windshield, lights strobed red and blue over the street, highlighting the squad cars and vans that clogged the small parking lot. Filling my lungs with a final easy breath, I left the air-conditioned vehicle. The air was hot and thick, the moisture hanging on every breath. Maybe that was why I didn't catch the scent of death while walking up the sidewalk.

The warehouse in front of me was little more than a dilapidated concrete block, faded red stripes painted on the top with a now-illegible logo. The dirty gray reflected the cruiser and ambulance lights with dingy brilliance.

I nodded at the various team members, getting only half as many responses. Might help if I learned a few names, but I was having a hard time getting to know this unit. At least uniforms still recognized me as one of their own; Stevens even graced me with a smile.

Just outside the massive double doors, the tech team was set up with stacks of evidence bags, several boxes of latex gloves, and other gear sprawled across cheap fold-out tables I saw at a beer pong party from a crime scene last week.

Harper looked over his shoulder, as though confirming my presence, before nodding to one of the smaller ladies on the other side of the table. "He's with me. Reynolds, meet my new partner, Gabriel Collins."

"Nice to meet you, Gabriel." The smaller woman waved.

"Collins is fine." I nodded by way of greeting. Only my mom had ever called me Gabriel.

"Got it." Reynolds handed me a set of boot covers and gloves, smiling curiously. "Switching partners again, Harper?"

"You know how it is." Harper shrugged his beefy shoulders, a grin lifting the massive beard that obscured the lower half of his face. Everything but his mouth, twisted in the usual goofy grin.

"Oh, that reminds me." Reynolds snapped her fingers, though the noise lost under her gloves, before rummaging through the contents of the table and producing a net.

Harper's face sagged and I almost laughed, despite myself.

"Captain says he keeps finding your stray hairs in crime scenes." Reynolds' dangled the beard net for emphasis in her slender hands.

He sighed and took it with the weight of the world on his shoulders. "Only for you, m'lady."

The girl broke into giggles and I couldn't resist a chuckle any longer. God, his English accent was awful.

I pointed to my chin. "You need one for me?"

"Nah, your stubble will be fine." Reynolds' smile drooped as she watched us head towards the door. "See you boys around."

There is no bracing yourself for the scent of death. No matter how many times you're exposed, your entrails always coil. Your brain does everything it can to cut off any signals that move your feet forward.

It's not as simple as the stench of finding forgotten steak in the back of the fridge. There's a darker element, something even more putrid than the human waste or the metallic tang that blood leaves in the air. Something primal makes every nerve scream, telling you to tuck tail and find the nearest exit in the least calm fashion.

Harper and I both paused, sparing each other a wary glance before marching on. Our footsteps blended into the chaos of coroners and field techs rushing across the concrete floor. The boot covers couldn't muffle the pounding feet sprinting past one another.

Most were working at filthy tables that lined the sides and middle of the warehouse, bagging scales or collecting samples of product left during the initial raid. A few went around laying out tiny yellow number cards or rulers next to the evidence they photographed before moving on. Moments later, someone else would come by, bag the evidence and label the bag before stashing the yellow card to be sure it wasn't used again. They were especially careful not to disturb the neat piles of white powder, holding every breath behind their masks while scooping cocaine into evidence bags and diligently labeling it.

A uniform approached to check our credentials and directed us with a hooked thumb. "All the way in the back. It ain't pretty."

I nodded and Harper thanked him. We found the least occupied walkway between two tables and squirmed around the team with muttered apologies. Towards the back of the two-story cavern was a row of offices. We could have followed the foul odor to our scene; the stench grew with each step.

Another tech was ready with expandable vomit bags like you'd find in an ER. He left no room to decline. "Someone already lost their cookies. Captain will have my skull if I let anyone else taint the scene."

We each took a bag and I pondered why I couldn't smell the trash bag full of vomit next to him. None of the answers that occurred to me were very comforting.

We stepped into the room. Harper halted with a strangled hiccup while I took in an involuntary gasp. The air tasted of death and decay. The riddle of the vomit was answered; a simple matter of force. The puke was being overwhelmed by a greater source.

No, not greater. Just bigger. Much bigger.

They were piled on one another, like crumpled scraps of paper in the garbage. Their limbs twisted in and out, the top ones cradling the lower ones. Protecting them from further degradation. There had to be at least fifteen but I couldn't count, they were too tangled.

What I could see of their arms displayed a constellation of puncture marks and tears. Their legs showed the same disarray, especially on the inside of their thighs, some directly on the groin. Their necks were all ravaged, exposing muscles and vocal cords under the thick ooze of coagulated blood.

Their faces were the worst. Some shocked, frozen in horror. But the most battered among them wore a petrified expression of relief.

Yeah, this wasn't just a drug case. Those weren't track marks from a massive overdose. These poor bastards had been used as human juice boxes.

I swallowed and regretted it immediately; the sour taste of decomposition, puss, and every bodily fluid flooded over my tongue. I barely made it out of the room before hurling my entire stomach into the bag.

Harper leaned against the wall behind me, muttering something I couldn't hear. Bitter acid built in my mouth with every heave.

One thing was certain. This was definitely a case for the Vampire Police Bureau.

One of the longer red curls tickled my chest, fluttering with her breath. Something in the simple sensation grounded me. Even more than her bare skin sticking to my sweaty arms as I held her.

Michelle pulled her cheek from my chest, her gray eyes becoming bottomless in the low light of my studio apartment. "What are you thinking?"

"I'm not." And I was enjoying it. All day, the scene had replayed on a loop in my mind. Every abused body and tortured curve winding in and out of my skull, only to return again. Sometimes mingled with images I'd spent the last year burying.

"Really, nothing at all?" She sounded miffed.

I tried to suppress a smile. "What should I be thinking about?"

"I don't know." The lipstick smear on her cheek twisted with her expression. Not a sneer but certainly not a pretty shape.

"Then I'm going to enjoy not doing it." I closed my eyes and settled deeper into the pillow. She sighed, laying her head back down, and started drumming those manicured nails on my chest. It didn't hurt. Didn't even scratch.

But it did make it hard for my mind to fall back into that elusive quiet space again.

After the fifth round of her using my chest as a keyboard, I popped one eye open. "Something on *your* mind?"

"Of course not." She smiled at me, drumming her fingers a couple more times before laying her palm flat.

Alright. I'd tried asking her and she wasn't answering. I could keep my mouth shut, she might naturally settle or finally broach whatever the topic was. I could also offer to take her to dinner, maybe getting out would help her restless soul. I wasn't sure what the best option was.

I wasn't in the mood to nag for answers; I had to do it at work all the time and didn't often have the mental bandwidth to chase answers in my personal life.

We'd only just started seeing each other recently. If not for running into each other at work all the time, I doubt I would have brought her back to this broom closet so quickly. Or maybe I'd just needed the creature comfort. But nothing in this space was likely to appeal to Michelle's standard.

She was in my arms now, I shouldn't be trying to push her away.

"Wanna get a bite?"

Michelle pulled on her prim little suit in a fifth of the time she'd used to strip it off. She had to hunt for her shoes. It took surprisingly long, given the size of my place.

I crossed the room from my bed to the kitchenette, pulling out a bottle of water and leaning against the counter. "I can't stay out too late."

She was on her hands and knees investigating under the bed.

"Oh come on. The *Alibi* is doing happy hour." She gave me a grin and bit her lower lip playfully. "I'll drive."

I snickered. "Pretty sure your shoes are in the bathroom."

The squad room was chaos, everything buzzing and swarming. Detectives were hard at work talking to witnesses, reviewing evidence, or writing reports the size of novels. So many bodies together in one small space and still, someone decided bathing was optional. My head pounded against the mayhem.

Michelle had wanted 'just one more' about twelve times throughout the night. I hadn't had any drinks, despite the temptation. The victims in that pile deserved a sharp mind. Not that I'd accomplished that, staying out so late. At least Michelle had been smiling when I kissed her goodnight.

I ran a hand through my hair and shambled towards the breakroom, following the smell of cheap coffee. The weak aroma did little to mask the diverse types of body odor. I pulled two flimsy paper excuses for cups from the plastic sleeve and filled both, leaving room for cream in mine. As a final touch, I snatched a stir stick and plopped it into the cup before heading back into the mayhem.

Harper was hunched over his desk, attacking his keyboard with the grace and speed of an old biddy taking a free computer course at the library. A crumpled coffee cup lay discarded on his desk.

"Riveting work?" I placed a cup next to the empty one before sitting at my adjoining desk and downing the majority of mine in a single swallow.

"Huh? Oh, thanks, pal." He sipped the coffee and grimaced. "Just writing up reports. I mean, really. I had to look through my texts to remember what time we were even called out and then check my GPS for arrival time. I still haven't gotten to describe that…"

He took another sip and his face screwed into a fowl face that couldn't just be the pathetic brown water in his child-sized cup.

"Heap?" I offered. There was nothing adequate.

"Heap," he confirmed and set the coffee down. "Have you talked to Don yet?"

"Just got in." I hit the power button on my computer, preparing for the mass of emails on new policies that inevitably developed overnight.

"Well, I caught our favorite coroner on my way in. Guess the majority of those poor sons of... those folks have records. They came up in the system when he ran their prints."

"Any pattern?"

"Mostly drugs and prostitution, a few petty thefts, but that's not what's interesting."

"Okay..." I had to bite my tongue. I was too tired for this.

Harper continued to scowl like his last sip had a bug in it. "There were a couple of informants in there."

I stopped typing in the middle of entering my password, peering around the monitor at him. "VPB?"

That would be something. Did our department even have informants yet? No one had arrested a vampire. We'd snagged the occasional Renfield but their tongues were always tied in impossible knots.

"No, not vamp crimes." Harper shook his head. "Narcotics. I haven't had a chance to review the files."

"I know a few Narc faces from my uniform days. You want to walk over and have a chat with them?"

"Sure." Harper clicked at his computer a couple of times before grabbing his coffee and standing. "Just give me a minute to grab some sugar."

"Which informants did you say?" Detective Amari clicked through his files, Harper and I hanging over his desk like a couple of carrion birds waiting for scraps.

Luckily, Amari remembered my help on a scene a few years back. Made it more acceptable to interrupt his workday. Though he'd thrown out a few snide questions about our life of hunting for ghosts and goblins.

His tawny face stretched with a smile; I tried to reciprocate while inwardly suppressing a groan. *Ha, like I'd never heard that before.*

Before the massacres, the VPB would have been the dream of a madman. Back then, Amari had probably thought drugs were one of the worst troubles society had. Now the war on drugs was a distant memory, barely discussed even by the highest politicians as the world acclimated. People were still panicking. After all, it had only been eighteen months since we'd discovered humans were not at the top of the food chain.

Harper rattled off five names, pausing each time so Amari could type and verify the spelling. Sure, we could have checked this on our own, but Amari could have the insider info on the detective each informant was assigned to. Might not be important, but the devil was always in the most unexpected detail.

"Damn. Two of those are mine." He let out a sigh as he scrolled through the list on his screen. "Rest were working with Michaels. He's on a stakeout right now."

"What can you tell us about your CIs?" I rolled over one of the chairs from an empty desk and sat, leaning in to verify the details on the screen.

I'd worked with Michaels a couple of times, he was a decent cop, very by the books. He hated to be interrupted. I had no doubt he'd cooperate with our questions later, though he'd be short. Based on records, he hadn't worked with his CIs very long. Amari, however, had worked with one CI for only a couple of months and another for over a year.

"Annie was a sweetheart." Amari thumped his desk with his open palm a couple of times. "I brought her in on charges of dealing but it became very clear she wanted out of the life. She wasn't dealing *contraband*."

He gave us a knowing look and Harper let out a nervous cough, his cheeks seemed to darken. I checked my notes. "This would be Annabelle Rogers?"

"Right." Amari sat up straighter and stopped his thumping. "Like I said, sweet girl. Shame she won't be able to see the other side."

"What about the other one?" Harper's tone held an edge I must have imagined.

Amari didn't seem to pick up on anything. Or at least he wasn't reacting any differently. "Jones fit his name to a tee. No one dragged him into this, he was just stuck in a nasty round of addiction and dealing."

"So, if his lifestyle was... self-inflicted, why was he informing?"

"Just a rat leaping off a sinking ship." Amari shrugged, his tone dripping with derision. "I had enough to toss his ass away for years, even if the prosecutor went in blindfolded. He didn't have a lot of options."

Harper pulled a small notebook from his leather vest and took a few quick notes. "Any insight into Michaels' group?"

"Never really interacted with them, though I could pull their files for you."

Pulling the file would save us time, plus it had the added bonus of jogging his memory.

"That would be—"

"No need," Harper interrupted me, flipping his notebook shut with a big grin that showed back to his molars. "I'm sure you've got a lot to do, and we can always view those ourselves."

It took everything in me not to glare.

Harper had just slammed the door shut. Anything besides taking my leave would now seem like I was questioning a fellow officer. Not a great way to encourage interdepartmental cooperation.

"Thanks for the help." I forced a smile as I rolled my borrowed chair back in place. "See you around."

"Yeah, I'll see you, Collins." Amri nodded, raising a hand to salute my partner farewell. "Nice to meet you, Harper."

"Likewise, buddy." Harper grinned and slapped the other detective with a high five just as Amari was about to let his hand drop.

Amari blinked several times, giving me a sideways glance. I shrugged when my partner turned his back.

I'd ground my teeth to nubs by the time we were back on our side of the building. "What was that?"

"Coffee?" Harper's grin grew even larger and he started towards the breakroom.

I let out a breath and followed him into the cheap vinyl space. He quickly found the cups, tossing me a couple of creamer pods from the top cupboard before shaking two sugar packets as though they were maracas.

"Thanks." I peeled the pods open and dumped their contents into the cup, watching it cloud the murky depth of coffee before their colors merged. "You wanna explain to me what you were doing back there?"

"You like Amari, eh partner?" Harper took a tentative sip of his coffee before snagging another sugar packet and shaking it. He was completely oblivious to the coffee slowly dripping from his beard.

"I respect the man, sure." I'd only worked with him on a few cases before transferring to the VPB. I didn't know him on a personal level, though he'd offered to start a poker night with me a couple of times. "But I think antagonizing a fellow officer might be a bad plan."

"He didn't even notice." Harper sipped, sighed in contentment, and started back towards our desks. It was still noisy and I had to stay close so we could hear each other without yelling.

"That's not the point."

"Did you notice the backpedaling?"

"Huh?" I went over the conversation in my mind. "What are you talking about?"

"He called her Annie."

"So?" Short for Annabell, made sense.

"Once I called her by her full name, his whole demeanor changed." Harper tweaked his bushy brows before sitting at his desk.

I thought about it. Amari's tone had shifted a little and he'd sat up straighter. But that didn't signify anything. He'd started by saying the girl was nice. He ended by saying it was sad she'd never see the other side. What was the big deal?

"Okay, well why not take his help with the files? Probe him for more insight if you're so suspicious?"

"Because, partner, I'd rather let him settle down so we can see what he really knows. Maybe it's nothing, but I don't want to spook him."

So, he had stopped questioning someone he found suspicious in order to find out what they knew...

Perfect.

"Sir, there *has* to be someone else." I felt like some whiny kid, and it was only compounded by the considerable man behind the massive desk in front of me.

"There will be, in a few weeks." Captain Murphy's shoulders were the giant blocks of a linebacker's, at least that was the obvious guess based on the wide arrangement of sports trophies shining in the huge hutch behind his desk. He finished tapping on his keyboard and turned back to me. "I'm sure you two will manage until then."

"I really think I would do better with someone else." How could I learn the ropes when my partner wouldn't even gather all available evidence?

The Captain quietly stroked the square line of his jaw, his glacier eyes simultaneously distant and locked right on me. I'd learned well enough not to interrupt this look. He wouldn't hear anything I said.

After another moment of contemplation, his eyes sharpened into laser pointers.

"Collins, do you remember what you said during your interview for VPB?" His voice wasn't chiding or even reprimanding. More of a gentle reminder from a family member trying to urge you to see the light. *Are you sure you want that career? Do you really think she's the girl for you?*

I blew out a breath and shoved a hand through my hair. "Yes sir, I do."

I'd told him about my family and hated every minute of it. Bringing it up always felt like I was trying to garner pity points; everyone has shit to conquer. But I couldn't think of another way to explain my conviction.

Most people trying for the new division wanted notoriety or re-sume padding. The Captain had to know there was something far deeper driving my request for the transfer.

This job was still the same shitty coffee, overworked hours, and low pay as every other detective position. Despite Amari's wisecrack, it was not chasing monsters down alleys or learning mystic incantations. It was sifting through lies and evidence, and seeing the worst of the world in order to protect the best. Captain Murphy had to see something that wouldn't wear off with the lack of glamor.

"When you told me everything, I assumed that a certain amount of passion would drive your investigation. That's why I gave you a shot, despite your lack of experience."

My shoulders slouched under the weight of his words. The longer I sat there, the more I felt like I was in the principal's office for mouthing off. Which was especially sad when I'd brought myself in.

"I assumed that passion would help you persevere." He raised both dark brows in question. "Was I wrong?"

I sat up straighter, the shame still pressing on me. "No, sir."

"Harper was the first seasoned detective to sign up for this department." Murphy grinned, the gesture further chiseling his marble features. "I'll admit I've had to make exceptions for some of his..."

"Excentricities?" I offered.

"Something like that." The Captain's grin grew a fraction wider. "But the man knows protocol better than anyone else here. He's seen us iron out some of the worst decisions from those idiots in Congress."

Translation: even if the Captain shuffled everything around, Harper's experience made up for my lack of it.

"So, do you think you can last a little longer?"

I chewed my cheek but there was only one answer.

I nodded.

"Good." Murphy gestured for me to leave. "Don't forget about dinner with the ladies tomorrow."

Some of the tension deflated from my body. "Like Michelle would let me."

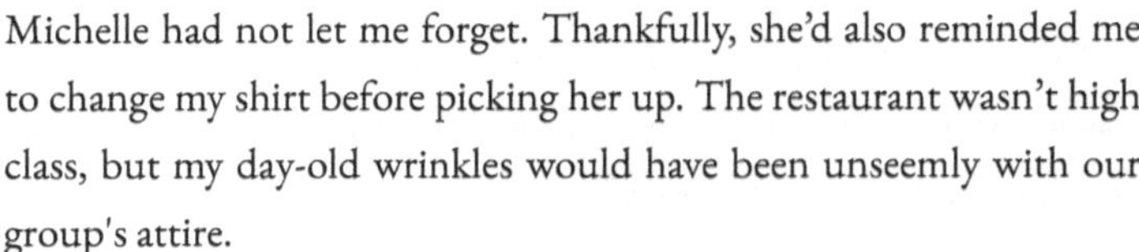

Michelle had not let me forget. Thankfully, she'd also reminded me to change my shirt before picking her up. The restaurant wasn't high class, but my day-old wrinkles would have been unseemly with our group's attire.

"I'll have the house burger, medium, please. And a Miller High Life." I piled the rest of our menus together, tapped them on the table so they'd be level, and handed them to our waiter. "Thank you."

"I'll be right back with your drinks." He nodded and rushed off to the kitchen, tripping over his ratty shoelaces more than once. Would he be able to stay upright while balancing drinks on a tray?

"So, where were we?" Barbara Murphy smiled, looking between me and her sister.

"Oh, give it a rest Barb." Michelle rolled her eyes but her grin grew while she absently stroked my hand. "A couple of dates does *not* make you an expert matchmaker."

"You can tell her that all you want." Captain Murphy moved a stray lock of his wife's hair behind her ear before kissing her temple. "Lord knows I've tried."

"Well, come on now." Barbara's smile sparkled in the low light of the burger joint. "I set them up, what, three months ago. And just look at them."

Barbara fanned her hands out like she was making a show of us while Michelle and I both exchanged a confused look. Murphy swallowed and took his wife's hand, running his thumb over hers. "You mean three weeks ago, dear?"

Barbara looked disoriented for a moment before that alluring smile returned. "Right, right. You'll have to forgive me. These late nights at the office are killing me."

"Oh trust me, we all get it." Michelle gave me a sly glance.

The waiter rescued me by coming back with our drinks. His delivery was so smooth I did a double-take to be sure it was the same guy. I took a long swig of my beer, trying to come up with another apology for canceling our date last night.

Harper and I had spent hours combing through the files for every poor bastard in the heap. So far, not one solid link to connect them all, aside from their mass grave. Our follow-up interview with Michaels hadn't been any better. His CIs were much the same ilk as Amari's. The thought made me take an even deeper drink before returning to the current festivities.

We'd all agreed ahead of time to leave the shop talk back at the precinct, for Barbara's sake. As a consequence, the conversation was simple. The kind of stuff soccer moms could discuss with their investor husbands.

Barbara wasn't dumb, murder and mayhem just weren't her cup of tea. Made me wonder how Captain Murphy had managed to court the jubilant kindergarten teacher. Either way, the change of pace was nice, if not a little disjointed. I could pretend to be normal, losing myself in basic details.

After dinner wound up, Murphy and I finished debating who was paying. He won the ticket but I insisted on the tip, even though either was a stretch for my budget. The Captain then kissed his wife softly on the cheek and scooched out of the booth. "Wait here, sweetheart. I'll bring the car around."

Michelle looked at me expectantly but my mind was busy spinning every gear. They were still grinding when I drove her home, despite the sour expression she gave me the whole ride.

The silence between us finally ate me up. "Let's pretend I see your point."

"Okay Captain Segway." Harper lifted his flashlight and gave me a quizzical look.

I scowled in the beam. "Do you wanna talk about this or not?"

"Don't get snippy, now." He chuckled and went back to sweeping his light over the concrete. "I've been waiting for you to come to your senses."

I bit my tongue, opting to check a corner of the room riddled with a spider web of cracks. The tech team had already swept the place with black lights and metal detectors. Still, sometimes technology just couldn't compete with the human eye.

That and we're desperate to find anything.

At least Harper and I agreed on this. But the team had been thorough. Our search hadn't yielded anything, even after two hours.

"So what changed your mind, buddy?" Harper took particular interest in the frame surrounding the doorway to this room. Part of me wondered if he really just wanted to be near the opening for fresh air. The foul heap had been removed the first day. Yet the stench clung to the stale air.

"Something a friend said last night." Or more precisely, Captain Murphy's tender inflection towards his wife. It reminded me of several conversations across the kitchen table as a kid. And just like that, I also remembered how Amari spoke of his CI. And I couldn't get that tone out of my mind.

"Well then, what would you like to talk about?" Harper was just outside the room now.

"Well-" I stood from my stooped position, my spine complaining after such a long time bent over nothing, "just for the sake of argument, let's assume that Amari is hiding something. Wouldn't it have been better to get all the information upfront?"

Following Harper, I found him scanning the remaining tables. We could have turned on the building lights, but sometimes little shadows or reflections caught your attention more quickly. A whole team of techs had seen this place well-lit, so we might as well try the focused sweep.

"Not if he's hiding something serious." Harper pulled a latex glove from his pocket, plopping the butt of his flashlight in his mouth before snapping the glove on. He mumbled around the flashlight for several seconds before spitting it back out. "And if he thinks he's still getting away with whatever that is, then there's no point in tipping him off yet."

I chuckled despite myself. I felt like Han Solo interpreting Chewbacca. Stranger still, I was following the muffled logic. "Alright, so you want to lay a trap?"

"Oh no." Harper picked in the crevice where the cheap table would have collapsed into one piece. "Amari is just the cheese for the actual rat."

He slowly pulled out a single piece of paper, a scrap that had slipped into the hinge of the table.

The squad room was still chaotic. Harper and I had spent the morning interviewing known pimps and drug addicts, trying to find a common thread for prostitutes. A couple had given us some good leads, but most of them were still our guests, courtesy of the charges we could prove for now. It took everything in me not to throttle one when I realized the boy he was trafficking wasn't even a teenager.

None of them were leading us to the vampire who'd started that mass grave; being locked up in our transfer holding only made them antsy. They had been expressing their displeasure in a variety of crude songs, cat-calls, and taunts. One thought urinating on a passing officer might secure his release. Said officer had commented on his shortcomings and kept walking.

Now, the pissant had resorted to howling. Amari had to shout. "Hey, boys!"

He was holding enough paper to publish an encyclopedia many times over.

"What made you change your mind?"

A chill ran through my intestines. I understood Harper's plan but I still wasn't excited about it. I hope it didn't show in the smile I forced.

"Just computer issues. Couldn't get them to come through on our end."

"Taxpayer dollars at work, am I right?" Amari eyed our adjoined desks, not seeing any obvious place to drop the load. "So, where do you want these?"

It was uncomfortable watching him balance the heavy stack but letting him drop the files would have been counterproductive.

"Actually, if you have a minute, we have a few questions about them." Harper grinned, his smile far more reassuring than I felt.

"Yeah, sure." Amari started to nudge the adjacent chair with his foot, slowly rolling it over.

"Maybe not here." I coughed and twirled my finger to indicate the surrounding space. "There are a lot of ears in this cornfield. "

It was a ridiculous joke my dad used to make; not sure why it came to mind. Still with the holding cell full of suspected Renfields; it wasn't a lie by any means. The legit dad joke didn't seem to put Amari at ease when Harper suggested an interview room.

"Oh." Amari swallowed a lump the size of a softball, his eyes flicking to five men howling some off-key musical number at the back. A timid smile crept across his face. "Yeah, sure. It is a little loud in here."

We walked down the hall, checking through the two-way mirror for the first empty room. Amari dropped the stack of papers with a solid *thud* on the metal table, rolling his shoulders and looking around the barren concrete room.

"Come on, bud." Harper's chair squealed in the tiny space as he spun it around before sitting down. "Have a seat."

I pulled the stack to me as I sat and started to flip through. Long reports, rap sheets, arrest records, and ongoing cases. Amari had been kind enough to clip the sheets for any individual member together, making it easy to skim through until I found the one I was looking for. He'd buried her at the bottom. I wasn't sure what to think of that.

"Let's start with her." I slid Annabell's file to the middle of the steel table, being sure to spin her to look directly at Amari.

"Okay, but I kind of already told you the important stuff." Amari rubbed the back of his neck. "Nice girl, wanted out. Sad but nothing new."

"We all know how it goes." Harper tapped the picture for emphasis, jabbing the poor photo with the broad tip of his index finger. "You see the person, good and bad. You hear their stories and their excuses. So, what made Annie a *nice girl*?"

Amari stared at the spot that Harper had tapped, as though he'd struck the girl instead of poking a grainy line-up photo. Even with the terrible quality she'd been lovely.

Many people scowled at the camera or cried as they held up their tiny identification placards. Annie's shoulders were slumped, layered in bruises. Someone had grabbed her pretty hard, otherwise they wouldn't show up in this blurry image. But her eyes weren't wide with fear or squinting with vengeance. Instead, she had this faraway look, her eyes off to one side, a stray strand of black hair clinging to her cheek.

Here was a girl resigned to her fate. Maybe it wasn't just the arrest on her mind at the time of the photo.

"Well, Annie was turning tricks to care for her younger brothers." Amari started to smile then dropped it, sitting up straighter. "Two boys, Jason and Alex, I think. She hardly ever ate but she made sure they always had food on the table. Even made sure they kept going to school."

"Where were the parents?" The words left a bitter taste in my mouth.

"Mom OD'd when Annie was nineteen. Dad was kept out of the picture and used for child support." Amari shrugged but his eyes were still locked on Annabell's photo. "I mean, that's what Annie said was going on with each of her brothers."

I gave Harper a sideways glance. He nodded. It was time.

"And when did you find this out?"

Amari snapped his dark eyes away from the photo, seeming to notice me for the first time. "Well, like Harper said, you learn things about your CI."

"Right." Harper stroked his massive beard, the shaggy mass blooming to life when he was done. "I'm just wondering if you learned this here in the office or maybe at the warehouse."

"I never went—"

"Or maybe he heard this after some pillow talk?" I gave Harper a sly smile but I was pretty sure I was laying it on too thick.

At this, Amari stood, slapping the table with both hands. "I don't appreciate what you're insinuating."

"Guess that makes us even, 'ey buddy?" Harper leaned his chin on the chair back. "'Cause we don't care for having a fellow officer hide things from us, do we?"

"Not so much." I shook my head, sitting back in my chair.

"What have I hidden from you, precisely?" Amari hunched over the table, his dark eyes turning black under the cheap lighting of the room.

Harper reached into his pocket and pulled out a tiny evidence bag, the crumpled scrap of paper smoothed out inside. "We found this while reviewing the scene a few days ago."

Amari snatched the bag, flipping it back and forth, over and over, before tossing it back onto the table. "It's blank."

"Yeah, that's what we thought at first." I leaned forward, pulling the evidence back to our side of the table. "But you know how protocol is. Got to run everything, even the trash."

"The tech team didn't appreciate the extra work on something as insignificant as an old receipt." Harper shrugged. "At least that's what they figured it was from the quality of the paper. Time and pressure wedged in a table rubbed out the content."

"Okay, so what of it?" Amari's tone was a bitter bite.

"Well, they dusted it for prints." I held up the bag. "Imagine our surprise when both yours and Annabell's were all over it."

"That's it?" Amari rolled his eyes. "I meet my CIs for coffee all the time. Not out of the question there'd be a receipt out there with both our prints. She probably dropped it in the warehouse."

"Oh, this isn't a coffee receipt." Harper grinned.

Amari's face fell into a mass of confusion. "It's blank, you said so yourself."

"Oh, it is. But the paper is more consistent with receipt from an ATM." I tilted my head. "Any reason you'd give a CI one of those?"

Amari's eyes grew big like he'd just taken Annabell's spot in the mugshot. There was that look of fear.

"She must have grabbed it out of my car." He stuttered, pushing out the words before he could stop himself. "We met there when we needed to be mobile."

"Oh, I'm sure you did." Harper smiled. "And I'm sure when techs are done with it, we won't find evidence of anything... how'd you put it, partner? I can't remember that fancy word you used."

"Untoward."

"Right." Harper snapped. "See, that's why I keep you around. Need someone smarter than me."

Amari looked between us, his eyes still growing wider. "You can't do that. I wasn't given a warrant."

"Pretty sure we can search the cars you've loaned out from the police department." I shook my head. "You probably wanted to keep a low profile, not drive around in the same car right? That's why you kept signing out the undercover cars."

Amari deflated, sagging back into the chair with a heavy thump. All the stress lines on his face vanished in an unnatural way.

"Just tell us why." I couldn't keep the venom from my tone. "Why'd she'd have to die? Why work with those leeches?"

It was a leap, sure. Amari wouldn't be the first to cross the line of propriety with his CI. Not by a long shot. But if he was working with the vamps, now was the time to find out. While he was vulnerable and unlikely to think straight.

Amari cradled his head in his hands, staring at the table like it was an extravagant painting. "It's all over."

Harper and I both tensed, giving each other a sideways glance before I spoke, "You can make it better. Just tell us how you got here. Anything you know about the vampires in Portland."

"No." Amari's voice came out with all the passion of a computer. His arms fell to his sides and his eyes lost all their luster.

The whole thing curdled my stomach. It would have been better if he screamed, professing his innocence. Anything but this sudden automaton he'd become.

I was trying to come up with a response, something to snap him out of it, but I didn't have the chance. Amari reached down and grabbed his sidearm in a fluid motion.

Harper and I flew back out of our chairs, mine crashing to the floor as we grabbed our guns, screaming for him to drop it.

"They warned me." Amari's voice was still monotone. As though his soul had already vacated the premises.

"Last chance!" I squared my shoulders and took aim. "We both know you can't shoot your way out of the station."

"There's one way." Amari jammed his service pistol into his temple. Harper and I both yelled something useless. The report echoed in the tiny room several times.

"You boys should have talked to me before interrogating a fellow officer." Murphy rubbed his temples, leaning both elbows on his giant desk.

"We didn't think it would go sideways." Harper let out a breath.

"Understandable." Murphy sat up and gave us each a tired look. "IA will have to review everything, so you'll both have to rock a desk for a bit. Plus the usual psych evals. Shouldn't take long with surveillance in the interview rooms."

"Understood." I swallowed, slumping a little lower in my chair. Harper gave a simple nod. When the Captain didn't add anything else, we stood to go.

"Collins, a moment please?"

Great, I was the new guy. He probably had a special lecture in store for me. I nodded and sat back down, waiting for the door to click shut behind me. "Yes, sir?"

"Those recruits are coming in at the end of the week." Captain sat back in his chair. "Given how this case turned out, I assume you'd like to move even sooner. I can shuffle things around next Monday."

The new subject surprised me. It took a moment for me to organize my thoughts before I spoke. "That won't be necessary, sir."

Murphy sat up straight, his brows lifting. "Really?"

"No, sir." Yes, this case had gone sideways. No, we hadn't caught our vampire and we had a mountain of leads that did not look promising. This wouldn't be the case to bring vampires to justice for the first time. But none of that was relevant to this decision.

"Well then." Murphy shook his head like he was trying to clear a notion. "Dismissed. We'll see you and Michelle for tacos next week?"

"Let me know if there is anything we can bring." I left his office, making a detour stop in the break room for coffee. Halfway back to our desks, I had to turn around to snag three packets of sugar.

About E.H. Drake

Visit our publishing website at http://www.ehdrake.com/ by scanning the code below for signed copies and free samples of other books.

You can also search for the E.H. Drake Podcast on YouTube & Spotify for video essays, free audiobook samples, and more.

If you love the cover, please check out our artist's website https://nicoleyork.com/, check out her amazing photography and artwork. Thank you again!

They've been there all along.

We never knew. But after the massacres, no one can claim ignorance.

Detective Gabriel Collins needs vengeance for the horrors they put him through. After two long years of chasing bad leads and false promises, he's starting to lose hope.

But everything changes when the vampire, Lily, saves his life. Now, Gabe has to work with his enemy. As he descends deeper into their world, it's becoming impossible to tell who he can trust.

Flip the page to enjoy the first chapter of *Blood Herring*.

"A good, strong start to the series that I can only see being built on." *Taliesin Meets the Vampires*

"...a great balance of well-loved tropes and originality..." Aisling Wilder, author of *Blood & Sand*

Chapter One

Paperwork. All the technological advances, and they were still burying me in paperwork. Each of my knuckles ached from the typing. I leaned away from the faux wood desk and pushed my hands through my hair. Off to my right, Sanders tried to coerce a witness into coming back. Sadly, none of this served to distract me from the case at hand.

This much typing should be considered cruel and unusual punishment.

In reality, I just wanted to avoid the rest of my report. I'd joined this department to help people, yet *people* were my biggest problem. Another case where humans were the perpetrator. Sadly, the stale ceiling tiles didn't offer any condolences, no matter how long I stared.

"Yo, Collins!" The shrill whistle of my partner made me jump from my chair.

"Jesus, Harper! You trying to get my attention or call back some hunting hounds?"

James Harper sat on my desk, holding a small stack of papers in one broad hand. His dark head shone in the bullpen's fluorescent light and pale flakes of Pop-Tart crumbs littered his bushy beard. "Sorry to scar you for life, buddy, but the captain just handed us a fresh one."

I groaned and eyed the already swelling inbox on my desktop. "My hands are cramped just thinking about the reports I gotta file tonight."

Harper smiled, shifting his big brows and burly beard, and spilling some of his breakfast onto my desk. "If only you had a partner to help with all those, eh?"

I stood, reaching across my desk to brush the pastry crumbs away. "Yeah and one that could groom himself."

My partner realized the mess he'd made and moved his big frame like something had bitten him. "Oh, shit, sorry, man!"

He dusted off the few crumbs I'd missed.

"Don't sweat it. Not many could brag about surviving the dreaded crumb attack." I shrugged as I finished flicking the last bits away.

Harper barked a single laugh.

My lips twisted up at the corners. "So, what's my next report?"

"Uniforms were responding to calls out in Rockwood when they found a body," he said simply.

My eyebrows knitted together. "That's not exactly uncommon for the area, what makes it one of ours?"

Violence, drugs, working girls. All of these were fairly normal for Rockwood, and we hardly got calls from the residents. We'd once had a woman who'd ram her car into her boyfriend's truck repeatedly. The next day, he'd dropped the charges, and I caught them making out in our lobby. Very classy place.

Harper handed me the stack of papers. "Read the calls."

I took the pages and began flipping through them. The skin between my brows pinched as I read the first anonymous 911 call. "Well then."

"Keep going."

I read on, practically shoving my nose through the paper. "Three different calls over four days, but all the same—"

"Yep," Harper smacked his lips on the *p* for emphasis. "And I guess the condition of the body was pretty gnarled."

I grimaced at the mental picture and handed them back to him. "Okay, let's go see if this is another fake."

Twenty minutes later, we were driving through Rockwood, and I was waiting for the twang of noir music to start. Or maybe my eyesight would slowly drift to grayscale as we descended into poverty. The bright yellow dandelions escaping through cracks in the sidewalk begged to differ. As did the expensive cars mixed among cheap lawn ornaments.

My breath turned into an exasperated sigh.

Harper flicked his gaze to me. "Something on your mind, partner?"

I debated letting out a good rant. The politics here made it so people had a hard time getting out. But then I would end up talking about the same people refusing to call the cops because many were criminals themselves. After that, I'd descend into rambling about the poor innocent kids who were quickly being taught that crime was the only way to survive and the endless revolving door of bad priorities and horrendous politics.

It would have been nice to blow off steam, but Harper had heard it all before. I decided to switch topics. "Nah, just thinking of the forms you left on my desk."

Harper let out one of his harsh laughs. "Hey, I bought coffee. Doesn't that earn me some kind of break?"

Harper turned down Lincoln Avenue and eased off the gas. Fast enough to move smoothly with traffic, but slow enough that we could watch for anything worth reacting to.

"A single cup isn't going to cut it this time. At this rate, you might as well buy me a new machine. Maybe one of them fancy ones with a timer?" The distraction was nice, even if it was temporary.

"Oh, and while I'm at it, I suppose you'd like it to be a fancy latte' thing with something for your— Ah *man*!" Harper pulled over and groaned.

A crowd had already gathered, some dancing on the asphalt in their pajamas or slippers, and even a few wearing house robes I prayed didn't fall open. This day was ugly enough as is.

"At least the news isn't here." I tried to give Harper a sympathetic look. Neither of us really cared for audiences.

"Yet," he grumbled as he climbed out of the car. "You take the scene and ME"

I got out and scowled over the roof of the car. "You're just trying to unload more work on me."

"Nah, I want to talk to the uniforms, see what they got." Harper walked off, politely elbowing his way past the onlookers and hailing one of the uniforms by name, "Hey, Johnson!"

I pulled a similar, though less successful routine, trying to smile my way through the crowd. Pretty sure someone called me a cracker, but it wasn't worth addressing. Instead, I rolled my eyes and ducked under the crime scene tape. It gave a soft *twang* as I let it fall back in place behind me and nodded at the nearest uniforms.

"Hey, Stevens, how's the missus?"

"She's taken a liking to ghost pepper pickles." He shivered in exaggerated disgust and waved me in. "How's Michelle?"

I shrugged. No need to talk about that here.

The garish light of the ME van and a couple of cruisers tried to compete with the sun in thick red and blue waves. The body was partially shielded under a red-splotched shroud as a stubby little man examined it. It didn't stop the putrid smell of death from wafting my way.

"What do we got, Dan?" I pulled a small notebook from one pocket, yanking the pen from the spine.

"I'm afraid it's the real deal," the medical examiner greeted me in kind.

"You sure it's not a fake, like last month?"

"Certain." The tail ends of his huge mustache danced under his mask like a couple of deranged squirrels while the tubby old looked at me through his round spectacles. He pulled the shroud back and pointed at our victim's neck. "Though the shoulder wound is huge, there are four distinct drag marks from the fangs. That's almost impossible to fake. Plus, this bite is the wrong shape for most animals."

It was hard to keep my neutral face for the crowd. No matter how many times you see a dead body, it's always horrible. The poor kid, couldn't have been more than twenty, was all black and purple like he'd been beaten before he'd been killed. His skin was stretched too tight over his face, like he'd tried to scream in his last minutes, but just couldn't.

Scenes of past victims swarmed my mind, trying to claim my attention. A girl missing an arm. A man being pulled at like a dog toy between two vamps before being torn apart. A mound of human pieces too mangled for me to identify.

I closed my eyes and breathed, forcing my brain back into the present.

"See, right here." Dan pointed to twin drag marks, the kid's neck sliced into big ribbons just before a softball-sized hole sank into the flesh. Blood had gushed in a reddish-brown torrent, making a nauseating congealed puddle on the blacktop.

"Damn, Harper's not going to like this."

"And you do?" Dan eyed me as he covered the kid back up.

It wasn't like I was thrilled it was a murder, but having an actual vampire case, that was exactly what I'd joined this team for. Not hunt down husbands who'd killed their wives with a damn deli fork. But the bloodsuckers hid their dirty business well, and I was stuck with a pile of human-posers. I sidestepped the question, "Any ID?"

"That was handled by uniforms."

Nice way of saying, *Not my problem.*

I took additional notes and shoved the pad back in my pocket. "Alright. Thanks, Dan."

Dan looked back to the victim. "Wish I could say it was a pleasure to see you."

I shrugged. "Come beat Harper at poker next time we get together. Maybe you'll finally have a chance."

Dan shook his head. "No offense, Collins, but I think I'll pass on hearing shop talk after hours."

"See ya next time, Dan."

He wished me well as I left. It took a minute to tiptoe back around the crime scene techs and the tiny yellow markers to make my way back to my partner. He was waiting for me inside the tape.

Harper blew out an exasperated sigh and combed his beard with his hands as I gave him the news. "Man...I was really hoping it was just another dog bite."

"Hey, at least now we know those 911 calls weren't fakes."

"Always looking on the bright side, 'eh partner."

Harper probably would have done all the paperwork from now on if I offered to go solo on this one case. But I needed him with me on this one. God knew what I'd find working a real case.

"We had to expect something bad when multiple people claim folks are disappearing right off the street."

It had only been two years, but in that short time, a lot of murderers had tried to fake vampire crimes to get away with it. God knows how many had succeeded, especially during the original panic. It took months for police departments to train their officers and medical examiners to properly sort the twisted fakes from the real deal. Sadly, most of my calls were for human-on-human murders.

"Well, Johnson—" Harper pointed to the uniform in question, "says they didn't find any ID and most people were pretty hush-hush when they canvased the neighborhood."

"Shocking."

"Yeah, but a few were a bit more adamant than others. They thought we should try those."

"Wanna see if *detective* puts the fear of God into them?" I lifted the crime scene tape to allow my partner through.

As it fell back in place, local news pulled up, the brakes barely applied before two men rushed towards the scene, giddy at their early arrival.

"Yeah, gotta start somewhere." Harper scowled at the newcomers. "Wonder why they left the body out in public. They usually seem to clean up after a meal."

Sad but true. We rarely vampire victims just lying around, that was kind of the problem. Vampires might eat like rabid animals, but they were smart. They knew how to cover themselves. Probably from centuries of practice, though that was just speculation.

The last time we found actual vampire victims, it had been a pile of working girls located during a drug bust. Their arms had been littered with track and fang marks alike, their pale and bloated bodies piled in a room for later disposal. That scene still clung to my dreams. The fact that we still hadn't brought in the ones responsible didn't help.

"I don't know. Maybe we got lucky and it's a young one." We walked up the street to the first of many houses.

"Yeah, I feel real lucky right now." Harper rang the first doorbell. Six slammed doors, a crazy old cat lady, a hoarder, and one house of screaming children later, Harper and I sat next to each other on a rather clean floral couch, sipping tea.

We both thought tea was a bit too frilly unless you counted the sweet iced kind. However, we'd both learned a long time ago that if someone let you in and you turned down their drink offers, they'd spend all their time asking repeatedly if you were sure instead of focusing on your questions. People's manners could be a damn nuisance.

So, begrudgingly, we both tried to smile and sip from our frail cups. "Ah, excellent, Miss Stafford. Thank you."

"Why thank ya, dear." The old lady's brown cheeks lifted in a smile. The tone complemented nicely the gray bun on the back of her head. "Now what'd you boys wanna ask about?"

Harper sipped again before starting. "Well, ma'am, we've received a few calls about unusual violence in this area."

"I imagine you already know that's not unusual 'round here." There wasn't any shake in Angela Stafford's voice but it had lost its sweetness. "It's one of the reasons I don't invite my children down here more often."

When I was a little kid, I'd thought of detectives as real-life super-heroes. They could crack any bad guy like magic. But then I grew up, joined the force, and started getting into the routine of interrogations. We don't have any superpowers, but the best detectives are damn good lie detectors. It could be as simple as a rushed word or a quick bite of the lower lip, but it didn't take much to set off our inner polygraph.

Something about this woman, how she talked about her kids, set the little bulb in my head off, bright red and on alert.

"Yes, we do. However, these reports were a bit more specific." I took another swig as I spoke. "We're part of the Vampire Police Bureau."

Miss Stafford's eyes darkened. She set her cup down on a doily covering the coffee table between us. "What are the vamp cops doin' here?"

"The VPB got word that there were a lot of disappearances at night with no traces." Harper put his cup down. It was well over half-full. "And I don't know if you noticed all the commotion down the street."

"Afraid I didn't. I tend to keep to my own here. I'm sure you understand. Little old thing like me in this area, I do best if I'm ignored altogether."

At her age, you only lived in this area because your budget wouldn't allow for anything else. Yet, when uniforms had come by, nobody had answered. The bulb in my head blazed brighter, but I kept quiet all the same, not wanting to upset the flow Harper had set.

"I'm afraid a body was discovered." Harper paused, trying to let that sink in. "We don't have a name, but the time of death was some-time last night."

"Ya mean to tell me a corpse done showed up in the middle of our street and y'all just now found it?" She looked mildly displeased by that, yet the volume of her voice didn't raise.

"It was a few hours ago ma'am," Harper continued.

She humped and sat back. "I suppose you can't watch this area twenty-four seven." She picked her saucer back up and began sipping idly. "I'm really not sure how I could help. Like I said, I mind myself."

"And we respect that, of course," I tried to sound reassuring. "We understand life in this area requires special precautions."

She eyed me and Harper over her cup, pausing on each of us, then nodded. "What do you boys want to know?"

"Did you hear anything? Maybe around nine or ten last night?" Harper took the reins again.

"I hear plenty every night. Guns a-blazing, little hoodlums yammering on at all hours. Just last night there was some hollerin' over there." She placed her cup back on the saucer and waved her weathered hand in the general direction of where we'd found the body. "Course, one could hardly call that out of the ordinary."

Harper and I nodded. He tried to prompt her further. "Any specifics stick out? Even just single words or names."

"There was a lot of cursing, yelling. I had to turn up Family Feud just to drown it out." She tilted her head and squinted her dark eyes at a distant point behind us. "I don't think I've heard that much cursing in my life."

I'd abandoned my teacup, making quick notes as Harper kept the questions going. "Any other details aside from the foul language?"

Miss Stafford pursed her lips and twisted her brows, trying to replay something in her mind as she spoke slowly, "Well...they hollered on about soda at some point."

Harper wrinkled his nose, and I stopped writing. "Soda?"

"Yeah, before I finally gave up and cranked up the volume, I heard one yell something about Cherry Coke. Thought that was weird."

Harper and I looked at each other. He looked as bewildered as I felt. We stood in silent agreement. "Well, Miss Stafford, I think that's all. But if you think of anything else, let me leave you my card."

"Nah, just write your number down."

Best guess, she didn't want to have a detective's card sitting around where her neighbors might see it. I obliged, tearing a page from my notebook, and handing it to her on our way out.

As we turned back to her on the stoop, I spoke loud enough for any eavesdropping neighbors. "Thanks again for the tea. Be sure to let us know if you do see anything."

She smiled. "So sorry I couldn't help but thanks for giving an old bird some company, boys."

With that, she shut the door. Harper and I shared a knowing look and walked away. We waited until we were back on the sidewalk to talk. Harper's dark eyes shifted back towards the old lady's window as he spoke. "Seem odd to you?"

"Yeah." I kept my eyes on the gray slab underfoot. "She didn't hear our ambulance arrive or a bunch of people talking over each other. But that old crone picked up on that argument no problem."

ACKNOWLEDGMENTS

Go to all my beta readers for both this and my debut novel "Blood Herring." Without your critical eye and sharp criticism, these stories would not be the same quality.

Copyright © 2022 by E.H. Drake

All rights reserved.

No portion of this book may be reproduced in any form without written permission from the publisher or author, except as permitted by U.S. copyright law.

www.ingramcontent.com/pod-product-compliance
Lightning Source LLC
Chambersburg PA
CBHW021601310726
48972CB00003B/899